Miranda
and the Frogs

by

Lucy Kincaid

Illustrated by Tom Hirst

BRIMAX · NEWMARKET · ENGLAND

Miranda is on the pond. She has her head in the air. She has her feet in the water. She is dreaming. Miranda dreams all the time. Miranda is paddling her feet. The frog is having fun. He is holding on to Miranda's foot. Miranda does not notice what the frog is doing.

Miranda has finished swimming.
She is climbing out of the pond.
The frog is sitting on her foot.
Miranda is still dreaming. She does
not know what the frog is doing.
Miranda is looking at the clouds.
The frog is having a ride.

"Can I come too?" asks his friend.
"Hop aboard!" says the frog to his friend.
What a bumpy ride it is!
"Hold on tight," says the frog.
"I am holding on tight," says his friend.

"Look at the frogs!" say the hens.
"Look at the frogs!" say the ducks.
"Look at the frogs!" says the cat.
"Look at your feet, Miranda!" says the dog.

Miranda hears the dog. She stops dreaming. She looks down. She can only see her toes. She cannot see her feet. The frogs are still having fun.

Miranda lifts up her foot. The frogs hop onto the other foot. "I cannot see any frogs," says Miranda. She puts her foot down. She lifts up the other foot. The frogs hop back again. They are having fun.

"I cannot see any frogs," says Miranda.

"Shake your foot," say the hens.

"Shake your foot," say the ducks.

"Shake your foot," says the cat.

Miranda lifts up her foot. She shakes it.

"Now shake the other one," says the dog.

So Miranda does.

"Be quick. Jump off!" says the frog to his friend.

They are too late. Miranda shakes her foot. The frogs fall off in a heap. The frogs are laughing. They are not hurt. The frogs are having fun.

"Now I can see the frogs," says Miranda.

Miranda has not got her head in the air. Miranda is looking down. Miranda is watching her feet. Miranda is looking for frogs. Miranda is not looking where she is going. She bumps into the wall. She falls head over tail.

Miranda picks herself up.
"Put your head in the air," say the hens.
"Look at the sky," say the ducks.
"Forget about your feet," says the cat.
"Carry on dreaming," says the dog.
So Miranda does. The dog sends the frogs back to the pond.

Can you find five differences between the two pictures?